SHAROO
TEEN QUEEN

ALSO BY W.W. ROWE

Eedoo Book III: Friends from Lollia

Eedoo Book II: Invaders from Blore

Eedoo Book I: Sharoo Awakens

Jerry's Magnificence

Jerry's Mastery

Jerry's Mystery

Jerry's Madness

Jerry's Magic

SHAROO
TEEN QUEEN

W.W. ROWE
BENJAMIN SLATOFF-BURKE, ILLUSTRATOR

LARSON PUBLICATIONS
BURDETT, NEW YORK

ISBN-10: 1-936012-94-4
ISBN-13: 978-1-936012-94-7
eBook: 978-1-936012-95-4
Library of Congress Control Number: 2020932798

Publisher's Cataloging-In-Publication Data
(Prepared by The Donohue Group, Inc.)
Names: Rowe, William Woodin, author. | Slatoff-Burke, Benjamin, illustrator. | Sequel to: Rowe, William Woodin. Eedoo. Friends from Lollia.
Title: Sharoo : teen queen / W.W. Rowe ; Benjamin Slatoff-Burke, illustrator.
Other Titles: Teen queen
Description: Burdett, New York : Larson Publications, [2020] | Interest age level: 012-015. | Summary: "Sharoo and Clyde are two years older than when Eedoo III ended. Their bodies are changing rapidly, and ruling Broan is daunting! In this sequel, dark magic breaks loose in the kingdom. Outing the sorcerer is too much for them, and Clyde is soon in mortal danger. To save him, Sharoo risks everything in a chaotic dimension beyond Plash's spacetime"-- Provided by publisher.
Identifiers: ISBN 9781936012947 | ISBN 1936012944 | ISBN 9781936012954 (ebook)
Subjects: LCSH: Queens--Juvenile fiction. | Imaginary places--Juvenile fiction. | Magic--Juvenile fiction. | Wizards--Juvenile fiction. | Rescues--Juvenile fiction. | CYAC: Kings, queens, rulers, etc.--Fiction. | Imaginary plac-es--Fiction. | Magic--Fiction. | Wizards--Fiction. | Rescues--Fiction. | LCGFT: Fantasy fiction.
Classification: LCC PZ7.R7953 Sh 2020 (print) | LCC PZ7.R795 (ebook) | DDC [Fic]--dc23

Published by Larson Publications
4936 NYS Route 414
Burdett, New York 14818 USA

https://www.larsonpublications.com
30 29 28 27 26 25 24 23 22 21 20
10 9 8 7 6 5 4 3 2 1

Each universe, however vast, is finite.

But the possible number of universes is not.

—Paul Brunton

DEDICATION

This unusual story, which dares to break briefly out of space-time, is dedicated to Paul Brunton, my wife Eleanor, and our grandson August.

Nearly all the action takes place on Plash, a small, exotic planet in a parallel universe. Any resemblance to other parallel universes is purely coincidental.

ACKNOWLEDGMENTS

Thanks to my wife Eleanor and to Sylvia Somerville for their numerous helpful suggestions. Also to Amy Cash and Benjamin Slatoff-Burke for their greatly beneficial feedback. And to Paul Cash for his invaluable insights, wordings, and wisdom. Any goofs or gaffes are my own.

ONE

It's a beautiful, sapphire-blue Twoday in Broan, on the planet Plash. Above the royal castle, fifteen dolphin clouds cavort and frisk. Behind purple bushes, scruffbirds squawk the arrival of large, white eggs.

Dolphin clouds were created many years ago by the awesome magic of the Wizard Wombler. No one knows if these playful fishlike clouds are living beings or not. Wombler also established the weird weather on Plash. From purple rain that tastes like grape soda to huge floppy snowflakes, you never know what you're going to get.

But today is sunny and clear. Thankfully, no glowing red spaceships from Blore mar the sky. No pale, colorful vessels from Lollia dot the Shipshape Sea. It's been more than four years since the hostile Glyzeans nearly conquered Broan. Three years since the vicious Morfers from Blore invaded. Two since the wily, evil Lollers arrived bearing deadly gifts.

Aided by her Floater Eedoo and the witch-like seer Mrs. Zaura, Sharoo managed to save Broan—and later, the entire planet of Plash! After King Kilgore and Queen Reeya were murdered, the famous young girl was elected Queen.

After that, Queen Sharoo made her boyfriend Clyde the King. Aided by their Floaters and Mrs. Zaura, they saved both Broan and Glyze. Now, they rule a pleasantly peaceful Broan.

≈≈≈

What is a Floater? An invisible, timeless presence. Something like a guardian angel, but also more. Little children in Broan are often in touch with their Floaters, but they soon stop believing in them.

Why? Grownups scornfully laugh. Having denied their own Floaters, they call Floaters a childish fantasy. A silly mirage.

Such arrogant ignorance is regrettable.

Queen Sharoo and King Clyde have contacted their Floaters through diligent meditation and generally virtuous living. They are deeply grateful. It's good to have a powerful force on your side, even though Floaters can seem frustratingly unresponsive.

Sharoo and Clyde have changed much through the past two years in relation to themselves and to one another. Their bodies are changing so fast they aren't really sure how to relate to all that's going on with them. Their thoughts and feelings about authority, freedom, and responsibility are evolving even faster than for most people their age—finding their own ways to what it means to be a king or a queen. Yet the relationship with their Floaters remains constant and nourishing and guiding. Unlike so many Broanians, they refuse to forget their Floaters. They even hope that during their rule they can help others remember and re-discover their own Floaters.

TWO

From above, on this glorious Twoday, the massive castle looks solid and festive. Its colorful banners ripple in a pleasant, steady breeze. Its gem-studded walls grandly sparkle. The Shipshape Sea laps the rocky shore below.

In separate bedchambers of the castle's royal suite, Queen Sharoo and King Clyde simultaneously awake.

Sharoo still has silky yellow hair with bangs, though so much else about her has changed. She's getting to understand more of what it means that her birth sign is the rare Silver Dragon, with all the complexities that brings. Clyde still has curly black hair and delicate, emerald-green eyes. He was born on the day of the Crystal Deer but can't yet relate that to anything that's meaningful to him. He has grown four inches and put on a solid twenty pounds. In Plash's low-gravity atmosphere, his arms and shoulders are developing impressively, and he's still learning how to exercise his kingly authority. He even has a little facial hair, which he proudly, carefully shaves.

"Good morning, Eedoo." Sharoo greets the air above her head, hoping for a reply from her invisible Floater.

Be alert today and tomorrow. Happiness can suddenly don robes of sorrow. The words sound softly in her head.

"What? What do you mean?"

Silence.

Troubled but still drowsy, she rolls over to catch a few more winks.

The Queen of Broan rises when she chooses, and not before.

Still lying in bed, Clyde greets Eeroo with a cheerful "Hi!" (He named his Floater after Sharoo when he discovered it two years ago.)

Beware. Your eyes may see what is not there.

"Thanks for the warning. But when? Where?"

No answer. Floaters will only tell you so much.

Clyde shrugs, jumps, floats to the floor. (Plash is a small planet, so gravity is very weak. The people of Broan wear heavy shoes.)

In his white-marble water room, Clyde refreshingly splashes his face. The warning, like a mischievous imp, hides at the back of his consciousness.

In another part of Broan City, a high-school girl named Blizza awakes. She is the granddaughter of the witchy Mrs. Zaura. The unfortunate girl was born with features that conventional mindmake portrays as quite repellent, and nothing has improved them through the years.

Blizza jumps from her saggy bed, floats to the floor, and shuffles to her water room. She squints at the familiar atrocity in the mirror. It looks so unlike how she feels herself to be inside. Snarling like a cornered tiger, the girl snatches up a jade hiphog. Glaring at the face she sees, she hurls the heavy ornament against the glass.

It makes a shattering crash. Splinters of mirror shower down.

"Blizza! Are you all right?"

"Yes, Mama. I, uh, was exercising. The weight slipped out of my hand."

"Well, make sure you clean it up."

"Of course, Mama."

Smiling grimly, the girl begins to practice her magic spells.

Clyde thoughtfully studies his bare toes. In the royal suite, his room adjoins the Queen's, and the thought of her so nearby makes him happy.

Still wearing his yellow silk pajamas, he soon finds himself standing beside Sharoo's bed. She'll probably shoot him down again, but it's worth a try.

"Morning, Roo."

"Hi, sweetie. How nice to wake up to— mmuf."

He gives her a hopeful kiss. "So is this going to be my lucky day?"

Sharoo didn't sleep well and is preoccupied with trying to remember a dream. "Clyde honey!" she says impatiently . . . "*Not again.* I've said so many—"

"I love you, Roo. We'll be married soon, and everyone assumes we're already sleeping together. If we're getting criticized for it, why not . . ."

Sharoo pulls her dark blue silk pajamas tighter. "No, Clyde. I'm just not ready yet. (They have asked the Council of Elders to change the marriageable age from eighteen to sixteen as a special case for them.) "And remember: Eedoo says it's better to wait until we're married. That discipline is important."

Clyde rolls his eyes. "That's what Eeroo says too. My Floater says that my desire nature must be controlled by a higher will. But I'm not so sure. We're the King and Queen. We can do whatever we want, can't we? Our will is pretty high."

Sharoo shrugs and wonders, alluringly stretching her pajamas without really realizing it. "Maybe," she muses, "if our desires are guided by a higher will." She raises up, gives him a careful kiss. "Clyde honey. Eedoo says the King and Queen should try to uplift each other and set an inspiring example for people to look for their own Floaters. That we'll respect each other and ourselves more if we wait."

Clyde nods. "It probably will be important," he acknowledges, "for us to respect each other as much as is possible. And it sure would be great if more people find and listen to their Floaters!"

But part of him is unconvinced. "Why did you make me King?"

"So we can be together, silly. But not *that* way just yet. I want you with me, and I don't want to be alone in this hard job. Besides, you know Mother Maura can't marry us in the temple until we get legal permission from the Council." (Sex before marriage in Broan is considered improper.)

Clyde is clearly dismayed. "But we've waited so long already to hear from them. Every day seems like a year."

"I know." Sharoo stretches. "But it's fun to look forward to it." She grins in an impish way that almost drives him crazy.

The young King nods. Smiling ruefully, he returns to his own bedchamber.

Left alone, Sharoo grows pensive. She loves Clyde so much! She tilts her head back and whispers.

"Eedoo, did I do wrong?"

No, you did right.

"Does he still love me?"

Of course. He loves you very much.

"If he ever fell for anyone else, I think I'd die."

You wouldn't die, but the recovery might be long and painful.

"Will the Council of Elders agree to our request?"

Very possibly. They are still debating.

"Are they upset because we don't wear those heavy royal robes?

That doesn't help. But it shouldn't make the difference. It is good that you both wear crowns.

"Thanks."

Mostly relieved, Sharoo begins her morning meditation, hoping that Clyde is doing his too.

He is.

She smiles. Eedoo easily reads her mind.

THREE

In the castle's morn-meal room, Milli and Bart are already seated. Milli has dark hair and darting beady eyes. Her sign is the Copper Cat. Bart is chubby, with a face like a boiled golden potato. He's a Ruby Fox, with a keen, quirky sense of humor.

When Sharoo became Queen, she invited them both to live in the castle. She also invited her parents, Ida and Wyfur Loo. They happily came but then moved to a comfortable cottage nearby "to avoid putting a damper on the young folks."

Another good reason was that Wyfur has a drinking problem, and temptations in the castle were perilously great. Just wish aloud for a tumbler of rye whiskey, and it's in your hand.

Most Broanians are happy to be ruled by two (or, the people suspect, sometimes four) precocious teenagers and two Floaters, but a few detractors snidely refer to the castle as "the nursery."

Now, with great gusto, Milli and Bart are munching a morn-meal of jumbled scruffbird eggs, bacon, and hot sweetcrusts.

"Morning!" Sharoo greets them as she and Clyde come in.

Under the table, Ruffy barks. (Ruffles is Milli's black sheephound. He came with her to the castle.)

"Morning, lovers." Milli slips Bart a knowing smile.

Sharoo blushes.

Clyde rolls his eyes.

Chief Steward Charlton brings in a tray with crystal goblets of mango juice, mugs of steaming coffee, and a plate of gooey cinnamon sweetcrusts.

The King and Queen order jumbled eggs and bacon.

While they wait, Milli asks if there's any word from Eedoo and Eeroo.

Sharoo hesitates. She doesn't want to say that happiness might "don robes of sorrow."

Clyde saves her. "Eeroo gave me a strange warning," he declares. "My eyes may see what is not there."

"I wonder what that means," Milli muses. "If something isn't there, how can you see it?"

"Beats me," says Bart. "But it sounds like the eyes have it."

Nobody laughs, but Sharoo smiles.

Bart clears his throat. "Why did the eye doctor go broke?"

Nobody knows.

Bart smirks. "He put up a sign out front: If you can't read this, I can help you!"

The others slowly laugh and groan.

Outside the castle, as if the weather is groaning too, thunder rumbles. Yet the sky is innocently blue.

The King and Queen exchange worried glances.

Ruffy whines plaintively. He seems to sense trouble.

Charlton brings in two steaming plates of jumbled eggs and bacon.

Everyone eats in silence. The sudden thunder seems like a warning.

Ruffy whimpers.

Clyde half-secretly slips him a bit of crispy bacon. He has a soft spot for the goofy sheephound.

Ruffy gulps, smiles gratefully. His pleading eyes ask for more.

Milli backs her chair away. "That's all I can eat. Bart and I have a rehearsal this morning. The play still needs a lot of work."

Sharoo nods. She knows it's an updated version of Shockspeare's comedy, *A Midsummer Nightmare.*

"Clyde and I need to preside over a C.C.," she says. "I heard there are some difficult disputes this morning." (C.C. stands for Citizens' Court. Broanians love acronyms.)

"The peasants are restless," Bart declares. "They might bring fitchporks."

Milli giggles.

Outside, in the clear blue sky, dark clouds suddenly form. Jagged lightning flashes. A strong wind howls.

Ruffy howls too.

Thunder ominously rumbles. Within seconds, blood-red raindrops strike the wide leaded window.

"Normal Plash weather," Milli quips.

Sharoo fearfully smiles.

The red rain descends in buckets now, dumped from a dark purple sky. It seems like a flood in the making.

"Go away!" Bart addresses the weather. "If you keep this up, it'll be known as the bloody rain of Queen Sharoo and King Clyde."

Clyde nervously laughs.

As if the deluge was listening, it stops. The sky abruptly clears.

"Look!" cries Milli. "You just have to talk to it."

In the sunlit royal gardens, the sparkling crimson liquid drips from bushes and trees—like bright blood.

Slouching in a corner of the castle's spacious kitchen, two servant boys converse in low tones.

"Didja see that weird rain?" says Auff, a tall lad with peach skin and shaggy green hair. He's already been into the mango brandy this morning, and his slurred words sound like "weir drain."

"Ain't I got two eyes?" asks Awn, a short boy with a zing-berry complexion. His words sound like "too wise."

"The King and Queen came down late to morn-meal," Auff says, leering.

"So what?" says Awn.

"So plenty. They were busy making the happy octopus, I'll wager." He winks lasciviously.

Awn absently picks at his acne. "But they ain't married yet. The wedding is still a good ways off."

"Who cares? They've got royal rights."

"Lucky stiffs."

"I'll say."

FOUR

In the throne room, the still-chaste King and Queen sit side by side. They wear white cotton shirts, blue pants, and golden sandals. Seen from above, their spikey crowns look like hair-filled circles of shiny gold teeth.

Like a bald, ivory-headed ghost, Chief Steward Charlton materializes in the doorway. "Pardon, Your Majesties. The first disputants are waiting."

Clyde clears his throat, hoping to deepen his voice. "Send them in."

No matter how silly the case, the Queen and King try to resolve it wisely. Disputants can be cranky and touchy. There is an old saying in Broan: "Your own skin is closer to your body." It means that your own troubles mean more to you than to anyone else.

Sharoo and Clyde often rely on acronyms like the L.O.B. ("Law of Boomerang"—Whatever you do comes back to you) or T.G.I.F. ("To Give Is Fortunate").

Charlton returns. "Pet store owner Mrs. Fritzi Fluff and Mr. Bartli," he announces.

What funny names! The Queen and King try not to laugh. Mrs. Flutz is cross-eyed and walks with a limp. But her dark-green face has an authoritative glower.

Mr. Bartli is a muscular man with orange hair and shifty eyes, leading in a gray-whiskered foon, tethered by a short leash.

On Plash, a foon is a cross between a fox and a racoon. Foons are very rare and brightly intelligent. But this one looks droopy and dull. She sits on the floor before the thrones and hangs her head.

"Describe your problem," the Queen tells Mr. Bartli. The man glances down at his foon. "May it please Your Highness," he growls, "I bought this here creature at Fluff's Pet Emporium. For seven gold crowns. She's supposed to be smart, but she's a bloomin' idiot! The foon, I mean." He sneers at Mrs. Fluff, who hisses with indignation.

The King smothers a laugh. He turns to Mrs. Fluff. "What is your side of the argument?"

The cross-eyed lady makes a fizzing sound. "Your Highness, pets quickly become like their owners. This foon was a genius when Mr. Bartli bought her. Now the poor thing is dumber than a humbug. The foon, I mean."

Mr. Bartli snarls.

The foon yawns indifferently.

The King and Queen briefly whisper.

"Leave your foon here for a week," Sharoo tells Mr. Bartli. "She will be trained together with ours. If she doesn't get any smarter (the Queen turns to Mrs. Fluff), you must refund the money."

The disputants bow and depart.

The Queen turns to Charlton. "Next!"

Two odd-looking citizens rush into the throne room. Charlton struggles to keep up. "Florist Herbert Verdi and Mrs. Rubi Hachoo!"

The King and Queen look down from their thrones.

Florist Verdi has a snout-like nose and little pig eyes. His skin is yellow, and he is very fat. The man has fuzzy green hair.

Mrs. Hachoo is extremely thin, with gray hair. Her sunken eyes seem determined. To Clyde, she looks like a skeleton covered with parchment skin.

"Present your problem," the Queen commands.

Both disputants start talking at once.

Sharoo gapes. The woman's voice is husky and deep, but the man's is high and squeaky!

King Clyde raises his ivory scepter. "Ladies first!"

Mrs. Hachoo smiles. "I bought two prize laffodils from this here dolt, Your Majesties." She growls angrily. (On Plash, laffodils are pink flowers that make a giggling sound when stirred by the wind.)

"And I watered them just like this bassturd said. Please pardon my language but it's fitting, as you'll see. After three days, when a strong breeze was ablowin', I went out and listened." She sniffs. "Them two laffodils didn't giggle at all. As prize ones, they was supposed to giggle like mad. But oh, no. They *cried and sobbed.*" She folds her arms, as if the case is closed.

"Kin I talk now?" the florist squeaks, his pig eyes indignantly gleaming.

"Yes," the Queen tells him.

"Well, Your Majesties, the laffodils weren't defective at all. Some people laugh until they cry." He smiles triumphantly. "So there."

Mrs. Hachoo glares. "What's that got to do with the price of peas?"

Verdi snorts. "Can't you see the similarity between a laughing flower and a laughing person?"

"Yes," snaps Mrs. Hachoo. "Also between a certain fat florist and a pig."

Verdi flares up. "Why you skinny old . . ."

King Clyde raises his scepter. "I think we've heard enough." He has no idea what to do, but this is going nowhere! Leaning back, he whispers secretly into the air.

Eeroo's answer isn't much help. *You must work this out for yourself. I can't spoon-feed you every little solution.*

Clyde nods, frowning thoughtfully.

Queen Sharoo, also whispering, is trying to reach Eedoo.

She encounters a frustrating silence. But then, her Floater gives her a crumb. *When you hit a dead end, use that good brain between your ears.*

Sharoo sighs with exasperation. That's just what she's been trying to do! These stupid disputes will be the death of her! She— Hey! Dead end . . . the death . . . Eedoo is helping her after all! "Thank you, Eedoo!"

You're welcome.

She quickly whispers to Clyde.

A grin spreads across his face.

"Take your sobbing laffodils to the funeral home," he orders. "Mr. Eboni will be delighted to have them appropriately sadden the atmosphere. He will pay you more than enough to buy some *non-defective* laffodils." Clyde looks strictly at the florist, who frowns.

The disputants bow and depart.

Charlton enters the throne room. "Beg pardon, Your Majesties. There is highly disturbing news to report!"

FIVE

"Disturbing news?" says the Queen. *Happiness can suddenly don robes of sorrow.* Eedoo's words echo in her head. "What is it, Charlton?"

"Flowers, Your Majesty."

"What!?"

"Beautiful flowers, Highness. A few have sprung up in Palisades Park. Lovely shades of blue and red." The Chief Steward sighs. "When people put them in vases, they emit a sweet but poisonous fragrance. Several citizens are seriously ill. Old Mrs. Birker is in morbacare."

"Praise the O.B.E.!" cries Clyde. "It sounds like dark magic. Are there any clues?" (In Broan, the O.B.E. means the One Behind Everything.)

"So far, Your Majesty, Police Inspector Columbine is baffled."

"Summon him at once." Clyde raises his ivory scepter for emphasis.

"Yes, Sharoo agrees. "Tell the other disputants to return tomorrow."

"Consider both done, Your Majesties." Charlton bows and withdraws.

Sharoo tries unsuccessfully to reach Eedoo.

But she has a strange suspicion. "I think it's purple magic," she declares.

Clyde gapes. "But Roo! Sorcerers haven't practiced purple magic for ages. I think Wizard Wombler put a stop to it."

"Well, someone is practicing something pretty bad."

The Queen and King pray for inspired guidance.

Charlton's ivory head pokes through the doorway. "Pardon, Your Majesties. Inspector Columbine is here."

"Show him in," says Sharoo.

A short dark-haired man enters. He wears a rumpled dark-blue raincoat and a black patch over his left eye. His face is light-blue. Broanians say he sees more with one eye than many people do with two. There's a rumor that he was a bloodsniff (bloodhound) in a prior life.

The Inspector approaches the thrones and bows. "At your pleasures, Your Majesties."

Clyde nods. "What's this about poisonous flowers?"

Columbine shrugs. "It's true, Highness. No clues so far, but purple magic is suspected."

"I knew it!" Sharoo jumps up. "What can you do?"

The Inspector gives a sly smile. "Sprout wings and fly?"

"Very funny."

"Forgive me, Your Highness. But my command of counter-magic is minimal. My badgemen are making every effort to detect suspicious activity. They have orders to apprehend anyone who might be magicking. Citizens are shadowed and scrutinized even as we speak."

Sharoo nods. "I suppose that's all you can do. King Clyde and I are trying to consult our Floaters."

Columbine sardonically smiles. "Excellent, Your Highness. May the sorcerer who did this evil deed be cuddled by a boa vine."

Sharoo shivers. On Plash, stealthy boa vines are half-plant, half-reptile. They hang from trees, swinging slowly toward their prey and then lunging. Their green, rubbery skin is sticky and very strong. They tightly bind their victims and gradually *absorb* their flesh. Hunters find clean white skeletons below these innocent-looking predators.

Clyde raises his scepter. "Thank you, Inspector. You may go. Keep us informed of your progress."

"Yes, Your Majesty." Columbine bows deeply.

Moving toward the door, he stops, pauses for a moment, spins around. His dark-blue raincoat swirls. "Pardon, Your Majesties. But doesn't the witch-like seer Mrs. Zaura currently reside here in the castle?"

"She does indeed," Sharoo replies. "And I'm about to request her *helpful* advice in this matter."

Columbine's lone eye narrows. "Yes, Your Highness."

He shrugs and departs.

SIX

Sharoo strides along the castle hallway, past gold-framed oil portraits of former kings and queens. Their eyes seem to stare disapprovingly, as if they wonder why the Queen isn't wearing her royal robes.

Passing the imperious King Kilgore and a serene Queen Reeya, Sharoo shudders, recalling their gruesome murders. Is she destined for a similar fate?

The girl hurries on, her face pale with apprehension.

Mrs. Zaura (whom the Queen also invited to live in the castle) occupies a small guest room in the east wing. And now, strange rumors circulate. Some say the cackling old seer has the King and Queen in her witchy power. Others jokingly call her "Mrs. Aura." There's even a jest that she was a scruffbird in a prior life.

When Sharoo knocks on Mrs. Zaura's door, three sharp barks ring out.

The old lady opens the door and smiles. Her single tooth gleams. "Morning, Your Highness. It's good to see you." (Mrs. Zaura seldom leaves her room; meals are carried in on silver trays by Awn and Auff.)

Mrs. Zaura peers up over Sharoo's head. "Morning, Eedoo."

The witch-like seer is the only person on Plash who can detect Sharoo's Floater, but Eedoo speaks only to Sharoo.

The Queen secretly wishes that she could see Eedoo too.

"I heard Sniffy announcing me."

(Sniffy is an imaginary dog. He used to bark when people came to the old seer's hut for readings. When she moved into the castle, Ruffy was baffled for a considerable time. But the Foon was never fooled.)

Mrs. Zaura cackles. "Old habits die hard. When I first moved in, my chambermaid Rinsa offered to walk Sniffy so he wouldn't stain the carpet. I told her he was trained to stand on the seat, hee. Come in, please."

"I have a big problem," Sharoo tells her, stepping inside.

The seer's face turns serious. "Doesn't surprise me. The stars are aligned like nervous spiders in a dark cellar. Please sit down."

Sharoo sits at the little round table with its familiar quarzz crystal. It seems like the witch's entire hut has been magically squeezed into this cozy guest room.

Mrs. Zaura touches a match to a lone waxlight. The crystal reflects its swaying flame. "Now tell me about it, Your Highness."

Sharoo quickly mentions the "robes of sorrow." Then she describes the poisonous flowers, adding that purple magic is suspected.

Mrs. Zaura thumps the table. "Curdled cauldrons! Purple magic? Let me have a look."

Sharoo sits patiently while the old woman gazes into the distance. Soon she has entered a deep trance.

After a while, Mrs. Zaura gasps. "Yee-ak! I saw very strong vibrations. It's purple magic, all right." The old woman sneezes.

"Brr. But the sorcerer's identity is strangely blocked."

Sharoo screws up her face. "Blocked?"

"To me, at least. Even the best seers run into snags. But I think this sorcerer is personally blocking me, as if he anticipated I might seek him out."

Sharoo squints like a surfacing smole. "I asked Eedoo, but he won't answer. I can almost hear my Floater saying: *You must figure it out for yourself.*"

Mrs. Zaura cackles sadly. "Keep trying, dearie. And I'll trance again, when I've stored up more energy. Perhaps I can find a way to penetrate the blocking. Or get a glimpse of your robes of sorrow. I'll let you know right away if I do."

SEVEN

At mid-meal, Sharoo tells Clyde, Milli, and Bart what Mrs. Zaura said.

Her three friends listen in rapt silence. Their fried-egg burgers and goblets of mocha milk sit on the table, untouched. Atop the meat, the eggs' crispy edges stick out from the buns.

"I think Mrs. Zaura will have an answer soon," Sharoo hopefully says. "She sees amazing things when she trances with her quarzz crystal."

Bart nods. "Quarzz is special. You don't wanna take it for granite."

Clyde groans.

Milli smiles. "I hope you're right, Sharoo," she says. "Whoever is practicing purple magic is obviously evil. And powerful." She shivers.

"That's right," says Clyde. "But what can we do except ask our Floaters? And pray to the O.B.E. of course."

"I haven't given up on Inspector Columbine," Sharoo thoughtfully declares. "I have great respect for his sleuthing ability. There's something uncanny about his single eye."

"Your one-eyed idol may be idle," Bart remarks.

Sharoo smiles, sticks out her tongue.

"I wish Bart and I could get in touch with our Floaters," Milli muses. "That might help."

"Are you meditating every day?" asks Sharoo.

Milli solemnly nods.

Bart nods rather casually.

Sharoo tilts back her head, whispers, listens . . .

Her expression turns serious. "Do you know what a paradox is?"

"Sure," says Bart. A place to park two boats."

Clyde snorts.

"That's funny," Sharoo says, smiling in spite of herself. "But this is important. One word: paradox. Do you know what it is, Milli?"

"I think so," says Milli. "Sort of."

"Eedoo just told me," says Sharoo. "It's an apparent contradiction that is actually true."

"Like seeing something that isn't there," Clyde says uneasily.

"Right." Sharoo reverently lowers her voice. "To get in touch with your Floater, you should recognize its presence as a never-absent protector. If you do, you will receive help from the O.B.E. But you will think, and act, as if you're doing it all yourself."

Milli furrows her forehead. "You do it, but you don't?"

"Yes. If you're successful, you will feel a happy peacefulness, a love beyond human feelings that holds you in its magical thrall. Eedoo says you must foster self-reliance even as you feel utterly dependent upon a higher power."

Bart makes a low hum. "So I'm a powerful helpless klutz?"

Sharoo tilts back her head. She whispers, listens, smiles.

"Like the O.B.E., your Floater is outside of space and time. But you must find your Floater *inside* your heart. Another paradox." She pauses, listens again. "Ego is the greatest obstacle. *Your* mind, Milli, tends to drift off into self-satisfied science-fiction reveries."

Milli blushes. "Eedoo seems to know everything."

Bart yawns. "Maybe my Floater . . . is a sinker."

Sharoo and Clyde stare at him in alarm.

"This is serious," Clyde tells him. "Your Floater can see into the future!"

"I know," says Bart. "But that's not my cup of tea leaves."

Clyde groans, throws up his hands.

Sharoo listens again. "Eedoo says humor is fine. And healthy. If a joke isn't malicious or mean, it can help to make others happy. But jokes aren't the best way to contact your Floater. Please keep trying." She cocks her head, listening. "You know how a handfighter practices his skill by breaking a brick?"

Bart and Milli nod their heads emphatically. That's easy to understand!

"Well, the best way to break the brick is when the hand-fighter focuses on the ground below it. And when you meditate, the best way to have success is to fix your mind on your Floater."

Clyde murmurs agreement. "I thought it would never happen with me, but it did."

Milli and Bart are lost in thought.

No one has anything to add, so they start eating their cold burgers.

"I'm not hungry," says Clyde. "Let's have dessert!"

Soon they are energetically tackling small mountains of mango ice cream with cinnamon sprinkles. For a few moments, they almost forget about any possible looming danger.

EIGHT

After mid-meal, it's time for Astronomy. When Sharoo became Queen, she resolved that her education should continue. A ruler ought to be wise, brimming with knowledge! For that reason, she and Clyde instigated what they call "The Double-A." Astrology, taught by Mrs. Zaura, and Astronomy, taught by Professor Wizzleford.

This Twoday, Astronomy takes place in the royal library, a large, comfortable room on the ground floor of the castle. Musty, gold-embossed volumes stand jammed into deep, mahogany shelves. The lighting is mellow but bright. Dark-green leather chairs surround a polished oak table.

At this table sit the Queen and King, Milli and Bart, and Professor Wizzleford. The man is a sight to behold! His fat head resembles a shaggy pear. A goatish white beard adorns his chin. His wispy white hair forms a fountain of fluff. And on his pointy, yellow-green nose, a pair of large square spectacles impressively resides.

Wizzleford spends hours with his powerful viewing scope. He knows exactly how the planets and stars are aligned, while Mrs. Zaura—who has her own way of accessing the cosmos—trances and intuits what it all means.

Today the professor takes a different approach. "Have you

ever wondered how life on this planet began?" he invitingly asks. His voice sounds almost dangerously friendly.

No one ventures a reply.

"Well, there are several theories about that." Wizzleford grins, clearly delighted to be spreading enlightenment. "Mother Maura, in her bamboo temple, will tell you that the O.B.E., in Its infinite wisdom, *imagined* our universe into being." He chuckles. "And for the faithful, that is all well and good."

Wizzleford clears his throat. Spectacles flashing, the old man surveys his silent audience. "Of course, there is also the T.O.E." (In Broan, that stands for Theory of Evolution.) "Like ambitious dolphin clouds, we allegedly evolved from the fishes and foons." He chuckles again.

"But for *thoughtful* people, it is not so charmingly simple. Some of us deep thinkers believe that in the distant past, Plash was visited by a scientifically advanced race of five-eyed aliens who came from the Twins."

Sharoo gasps. Beyond the Fighting Warrior, the Winged Horse, and the Little Dripper, in the far reaches of the universe, the Twins can only be seen with the professor's powerful viewing scope. These two distant stars are called Caster and Pollen.

Wizzleford proudly grins. "These amazing five-eyed aliens actually sowed our original seeds. Since that time, they have monitored and subtly guided our scientific progress."

Clyde whistles.

Milli's beady eyes sparkle. "I read that article!" she says excitedly. "Two years ago, in an issue of *Mind-Chilling Speculations*."

Wizzleford turns bright pink.

"I love that magazine!" Milli exclaims. "They had a cool story about telepathic turnips. And one about monsters with slimy green teeth!"

Professor Wizzleford mops his forehead with a light-blue handkerchief. "What a remarkable coincidence," he mutters hastily. "I'll have to take a look at that magazine. It sounds interesting." He mops some more. "Well, that's all for today. Your assignment for next week is to read chapter eleven of your astronomy texts."

NINE

The rest of Twoday is uneventful. No responses from either Floater. No more blood-red rain. No word from Mrs. Zaura.

In Palisades Park, Inspector Columbine's badgemen are grimly posted. They have strict orders to stop anyone from picking the lovely, evil flowers which magically spring up again as soon as they are plucked.

Watching from a safe distance, Broanians guardedly whisper.

"Those flowers sure are pretty!" says Mrs. Lorkins, a gray-haired woman in a lacy pink blouse. "Look! They've turned their petals toward us! They remind me of the nosebright Elmer used to bring me on our anniversary." Her hands are itching to pick a few.

"Don't you be fooled, Sarah," says Tilli Furlom. "Julia Birker is in the horse spittle." She grins at her wicked little joke. "I never did like Julia much, but still."

"For shame, Tilli." Mrs. Lorkins frowns reproachfully, but she squeamishly retreats.

The lovely flowers have lost their allure.

Late in the afternoon, the citizens of Broan collectively gasp.

An ominous "imp-flames" sunset is slowly forming behind

the purple forests and fields! This odd celestial display resembles bright orange flames with sly, imp-like faces.

Like grinning, living beings, the flame-faces flicker and bob. Broanians gape, murmuring fearfully.

The gleeful imps seem aware of a terrible danger, soon to materialize. The eerie light of the orange flames is lovely, but as everyone knows, this rare sunset inevitably portends disaster.

The weather on Plash is often weird, but never wrong.

Watching from a castle window, Sharoo shudders. Once again, she recalls Eedoo's warning about "robes of sorrow."

The imp-flames sunset gives rise to anxious whispers among elder Broanians.

"Oh, woe!" Mr. Tarnickel fearfully croaks, running bony fingers through his thin white hair. "I remember the thirty-day flood, predicted by the very same sort of sunset!"

"That was nothing!" whispers ancient Mrs. Morzh. "All we needed then was boats." She's confined to a wheelchair, but her rheumy eyes glisten fiercely in her wrinkled bluish face.

"Fifteen years before that, imp-flames foretold the horrid F.Y.I." (This stands for Flesh-eating Yellow Infestation.) "More than four hundred people died! If a sorcerer named Korzil hadn't discovered that snoots are an antidote, everyone in Broan might have perished. People were running about with their faces falling off." (In Broan, "snoots" are sweet yellow berries that grow on bushes with sticky prickers.)

In the servants' quarters of the castle, Awn and Auff fearfully converse.

"Remember old Mr. Squirk?" says Auff, scratching his shaggy green head.

"Sure do," Awn replies, fingering his acne. "The poor gent was takin' an innocent walk in the woods and got grabbed by a boa vine in the dark. It happened soon after an imp-flames sunset."

"That's right," says Auff, grimacing. "There wasn't much left when they cut him down three days later."

"Ugh," says Awn.

At eve-meal, the bright dining hall doesn't seem as cheerful as usual. Even the flickering waxlights appear to have lost their mellow splendor.

Milli excitedly mentions the imp-flames sunset. "I wonder what it predicted," she fearfully muses.

Bart smirks. "Maybe an impudent imposter will imperil us." Nobody laughs.

Nibbling an egg-slice spread with caviar, Sharoo tells Milli and Bart about the poisonous flowers.

"Maybe *that* was it!" cries Milli.

"No," Clyde tells her. "The poisonous flowers happened before the sunset."

Bart smirks. "How do you cure a case of poison ivy?"

No one says a word.

"You start from scratch."

Millie smothers a giggle.

"And how do you make a witch scratch?" Bart pauses a beat. "Remove her "w.""

Clyde rolls his eyes, snickers.

Sharoo frowns. "That's enough, Bart. This is serious."

"Yes," says Clyde. "They took Mrs. Birker to morbacare. Sharoo and I summoned Inspector Columbine, but he doesn't have a clue about the flowers."

"He ought to," says Bart. "With *his* name."

"No more, Bart!" Sharoo slams down her fork. But she's hiding a smile. Bart, she thinks, can be too clever for his own good.

"Why don't you ask Mrs. Zaura about the flowers?" says Milli.

"I did," Sharoo replies. "She went into a trance and confirmed that it's purple magic."

"Eee!" Milly cries. "Who's doing it?"

Sharoo shrugs. "She tried to find out, but the sorcerer is personally blocking her."

"That's weird," Milli murmurs.

"Mrs. Zaura has never failed me before," says Sharoo. "And she's going to trance some more. Evidently, the sorcerer *anticipated* that she'd try to seek him out . . . and prepared for it."

Bart whistles. "Maybe the sorcerer's sore at her."

No one even smiles.

TEN

Threeday dawns drizzly and foggy. Broan City is abuzz with speculations about the red rain and the ominous imp-flames sunset.

Seen from above, the castle's slate roof dully shines. The banners depicting a silver dragon and a mountain hang like limp rags.

In another part of the city, Blizza opens her eyes. Recalling the menacing sunset, she grins. The orange display was a futile attempt to warn her victims. But it's too late now.

She springs from her bed, floats to the floor.

Soon the girl is grimly at work. On her desk lie two little dolls, made from cardboard and fragments of cloth. They look remarkably like Clyde and Sharoo.

Sharoo awakens in her luxurious bed, gazes up at the inscrutable ceiling. "Morning, Eedoo."

Silence.

"Were the 'robes of sorrow' the poisonous flowers?"

More silence. Eedoo can be very stubborn.

"Did the imp-flames sunset mean that the sorrow is yet to happen?"

Yes. I meant something ... closer to you than the flowers. You will know when and if the sorrow occurs.

"Yikes! What can I do?"

Resounding silence.

"Wasn't Professor Wizzleford silly?"

Sadly mistaken. Humans outwardly seem to evolve, but they actually unfold in an inner reality. The professor's condescending mocking of Mother Maura contained some truth.

"You mean, when he said the O.B.E. imagined our universe into being?"

Yes. The only ultimate reality is the realm of the O.B.E. The best way to try to picture it ... is to think about what it is not. No space. No time. No person observing.

Sharoo smiles. "A paradox to us."

Right.

"Thanks." Sharoo throws back the covers, and jumps. She floats to the floor, shuffles to her lavish marble water room.

Water rituals completed, she meditates, sitting cross-legged on a gold cushion on the floor. A.S.A.P.—Alert, Still, And Poised. Sharoo made up that one. Slow, deep breaths ...

In his bedchamber, Clyde opens one eye. "Morning, Eeroo."

Good morning.

"Can you give me a clue about what will happen today?"

No.

"I'm the King, you know. It might help me save the kingdom. In case of a dire emergency. Will my eyes see 'what is not there' today?"

The future isn't set in stone. There is a strong possibility that it will happen soon.

"Can you tell me anything more?"

Remember mindmake? Your conscious mind creates an idea of the world based on what your eyes and other senses report.

"Is that all you can tell me?"

Yes.

"Thanks!" Clyde reluctantly trudges to his water room. "Was I too sarcastic?" he wonders.

No.

Soon he is perched on a pillow, intently meditating.

Morn-meal is somber. Today, everyone has scromelets (scruff-bird-egg omelets) with dollops of cinnamon-banana jam.

Chef Sooful has sprinkled his creations with chocolate nutmeg, but the scromelets go unpraised. The four teenagers eat languidly, sipping goblets of mango juice in silence. Even Bart doesn't venture to joke.

Milli says their play rehearsal is scheduled for the afternoon. Sharoo and Clyde prepare for Citizens' Court.

Soon the Queen and King sit imperiously on their thrones.

"All right, Charlton!" Sharoo calls. "We're ready."

The Chief Steward ushers in a gray-haired farmer with a purple hayseed in his teeth. He needs a shave. Behind him shuffles a dapper man in starched white clothes with a puffy white stovepipe hat.

"Farmer Hipswitch and Chef Morgan Tang!"

The Queen leans forward. "State your complaint," she tells the farmer.

"It ain't me, Your Highness. I'm real peaceable like." He gestures at the chef. "It's that confounded cook. He's got a hornet in his hat."

Sharoo turns to Mr. Tang. "Well?"

The chef makes a sweeping bow. "May it please Your Majesties, I am the owner of Morgan's Morn-meal, where the elite eat. My jumbled eggs could be served without a qualm to Your Highnesses yourselves." He smiles proudly. "I have been buying scruffbird eggs from this, uh, gentleman for some time. We have a contract too, all legal and such."

"Get to the point," orders the King.

"Of course, Your Highness." The chef smiles. "Well, the eggs were fine until recently. For all I know, Hipswitch has started feeding his scruffbirds white soap flakes please pardon the sickening thought."

"The point!" says Clyde.

"Of course. Well, I crack open an egg, and the yolk is white. All of them are like that. As Your Highnesses can imagine, my famous jumbled eggs are now chalk-white. People think they're sickeningly pale, even though they taste the same. My faithful customers now go to Cori's Café." He scowls bitterly.

The Queen looks down at Farmer Hipswitch. "Did you change the scruffbirds' diet?"

"Praise the O.B.E., no!" The hayseed flutters from the farmer's mouth. "May it please Your Majesties," he adds. "The white yolks just happened." He lowers his voice. "I fear it was the imp-flames sunset."

"Impossible!" Chef Tang exclaims. "The chalk-colored yolks have happened for several days now."

"That's enough," King Clyde tells them.

He and Queen Sharoo try to consult their Floaters.

There is no voiced reply, but the Queen suddenly has an idea. A totally unexpected idea.

"Put a big sign in your window," she tells Mr. Tang. Have it read: *Fresh jumbled eggs! No artificial coloring added.*

The cook's mouth falls open. He smiles a crafty smile. "That just might work. Thank you, Your Majesty!"

"And keep paying this farmer the price you agreed upon."

"Yes, Your Highness."

The two disputants happily depart.

Charlton rushes breathlessly into the throne room. "Another crisis, Your Majesties!" His ivory face is pinkly flushed. His hands are shaking. His bulging eyes are wild.

ELEVEN

Charlton stands before the Queen and King in horrified silence.

The Queen straightens up on her throne. "What is it now?"

"Puppies, Your Highness."

Sharoo gapes. "What!?"

"Puppies. Cute, winsome ones. They appear in gardens and on doorsteps. People take them in, adopt them, and before long, they become savage monsters." Charlton pauses. "Purple magic is suspected again."

Sharoo frowns. "What kind of monsters?"

"The puppies change color, Your Majesty. They become deep green. They grow spikes on their heads. And long, sharp fangs. Mrs. Kranderhof was viciously bitten. 'He was so darling!' she moaned. The badgemen rushed her to the hospital. She has seven stitches in her nose."

"Praise the O.B.E.! I hope they gave her numbapain."

"I presume so, Your Highness."

The Queen rises. "No more disputants today."

"Yes, Your Majesty."

"You may leave. The King and I . . . will handle this."

"Yes, Highness."

Sharoo turns to Clyde. "Let's meditate. Our Floaters have simply got to help us with this one!"

"All right," says Clyde. "But maybe Mrs. Zaura has discovered something."

"I don't think so," Sharoo replies. "She'd have let me know."

The Queen and King meditate on their thrones. They beseech their Floaters for a way to stop the spreading disasters. They also pray to the O.B.E.

Absolute silence.

Mid-meal is somber. Outside the window, it's still dark and drizzly.

Bart cracks a joke about a smug smog that flops.

Everyone is worried about the poisonous flowers especially because of the blood-red rain and imp-flames sunset.

Over large portions of cinnamon coconut ice cream, Sharoo tells Milli and Bart about the treacherous puppies.

"That's awful!" Milli exclaims. "I love to hug puppies. It sounds like someone with purple magic has read too many issues of *Mind-Chilling Speculations.*"

"Don't forget the flowers," says Bart. "The laffodil dispute *and* the evil flowers in the park. There's a lot of emphasis on bloom and gloom now." He pauses thoughtfully. "They both rhyme with doom."

Sharoo shudders.

Returning to their thrones, Sharoo and Clyde meditate and pray again, seeking answers. They ask humbly, earnestly, desperately.

A frustrating silence descends.

"My mind's a blank," says Clyde. "Let's watch some of the *Midsummer Nightmare* rehearsal."

"Good idea." Sharoo winks. "Maybe the farce will get your mind off making love for a while!"

Clyde nods. "There's so much gloom, I wasn't even thinking about that. For once."

Sharoo draws herself up. "Charlton!" she calls. "Summon the royal carriage!"

The Chief Steward's ivory bald head appears in the doorway. "Yes, Your Highness. Right away."

In two shakes of a foon's tail (as Broanians like to say), the shiny gold carriage—drawn by four snorting horses—pulls up to the castle. The steeds whinny, hoofing the wet roadway in place. They seem invigorated by the light drizzle.

Sharoo and Clyde emerge from the huge castle door. Seen from above, their gold crowns sparkle in the rain.

Waiting just outside, Awn and Auff scramble to hold brellas above the royal couple. They seem awkward and clumsy. Mango brandy is warming on a rainy day. Breath mints conceal the transgression.

Charlton swings open the carriage door with the black B painted on it. Loop, the dark-green, wolf-faced coachman, nods chummily. (He has replaced Zoop, who was killed together with Queen Reeya and King Kilgore. Loop could easily have been a wolf in a prior life.) "Where to, Your Majesties?"

"Speare Theater," Clyde replies. "And hurry!"

Loop gapes. "Are you jesting, Your Majesty? It's only a few blocks away." He brays like a dim-witted donkass. He's also had a few slugs of mango brandy.

Clyde frowns. "It's raining, Loop. Are you serious about keeping your job?"

The coachman's wolf-eyes widen. "Yes, Your Highness! I love my job. A thousand pardons. Yee-yap!"

TWELVE

The royal carriage pulls up to Speare Theater. This round modern building looks like a giant red apple. It has four white marble pillars, two on each side. It was designed by the famous architect, Frank L. Bright.

The rain abruptly abates, as if restrained by benevolent deities.

"Well, something's going right," Sharoo remarks. The phrase *Robes of Sorrow* still weighs upon her mind. She needs to stay alert!

The King and Queen enter the darkened theater. Avoiding the royal balcony, they sink into plush seats up close to the stage. The rehearsal is in full swing.

Grinning imps, dressed in skintight green costumes, scamper onto the narrow forestage. Behind them, a painted curtain displays leafy purple trees.

The imps chortle fiendishly. Two of them drag out a black cardboard cauldron. It has red-orange flames painted on the bottom.

With a long wooden spoon, a tall imp stirs the giant pot.

Like sprightly, cavorting fairies, the imps dance around the cauldron, singing:

Spirits, swirling like an ocean!

Hark our cunning, roguish notion.

Help us brew this passion potion.

The forest-curtain parts, revealing a dim-lit saloon.

Bart stands at the dark wooden bar, clutching a pewter mug.

Bart is playing Delusio, a portly nobleman in a pearled jerkin. The villainous barkeep Perfidio, played by a greasy-haired peasant, smiles. (As Sharoo and Clyde know, Bart's ale is laced with the imps' potion. It will cause Delusio to fall in love with the first person he sees.)

Into the shadowy saloon saunters . . . The Foon! Dressed in tattered rags, the clever animal approaches the bar on his hind legs.

The Foon is played by the Foon.

In no time at all, Bart is begging to kiss the snooty animal. The Foon haughtily rejects his advances.

Bart's faithful, bewildered girlfriend Loyola enters. She is played by Milli. Dismayed, Loyola waves her arms, melodramatically wailing.

Bart falls to his knees, fondly reciting a poem. "I love you, Foon, beyond all measure. You are my love, my life, my treasure . . ."

The Foon aloofly sniffs the air.

Milli continues to wave and wail.

Sharoo and Clyde laugh merrily. It's funny to see their friends in such silly roles.

All of a sudden, the theater trembles and shakes. The very air seems to shiver and shimmer.

"Help! It's a plashquake!" Milli screeches.

"That's not the right line," says Bart. But he too is terrified. Everyone is frozen, braced for another rumbling tremor.

Fortunately, the quake is over as quickly as it hit.

"Whew!" says Clyde. "I thought the theater would collapse."

"Thank the O.B.E. it didn't," says Sharoo, breathing with relief.

Amazingly, there is no damage!

After a few minutes, the rehearsal intrepidly continues.

Into the barroom saunters Allura, a seductress. She is played by a high school student named Blizza. It's amusing because her facial features appear so ugly.

Blizza's yellow-orange skin is dotted with light-brown warts. Her long nose curves down close to thick purple lips. Her eyes glow like hot coals.

"Her makeup is great," whispers Clyde, laughing.

"No makeup," Sharoo tells him. "She's Mrs. Zaura's granddaughter."

Clyde's eyes grow wide.

"I feel sorry for her," Sharoo declares.

On stage, when the Foon spell wears off, Blizza magically enchants Bart, who humorously woos her. Devastated, Loyola wails again. Bart masterfully feigns adoration of Blizza's ugliness.

The play ends when Blizza accidentally drinks some of the passion potion and falls in love with the Foon. Bart still pursues Blizza, who is chasing the Foon as the curtain falls.

Sharoo laughs uneasily. She feels sorry for the ugly girl. "Clyde," she says, "please go backstage and tell Blizza what a wonderful actress she is."

Clyde nods. "Sure."

THIRTEEN

Clyde knocks on Blizza's dressing-room door.

"Just a second! Keep your fingers on!" Blizza's voice is scratchy and sharp.

Clyde patiently waits.

When the little door swings open, he is flabbergasted. He stands face to face with a breathlessly beautiful girl! He can't believe his eyes. "Hello, I thought this was Blizza's dressing room . . ."

"I'm Blizza, may it please Your Majesty." She looks him piercingly in the eyes.

Clyde feels a wave of pleasant dizziness. He is dazzled, bewitched. Murky waves of purple magic encircle him. His deep love for Sharoo is sealed in a tight, remote container.

"Please come in." Blizza's harsh voice is soft and seductive now.

Clyde rubs his eyes, follows her into the dressing room.

Blizza slyly smiles. Influenced by purple magic, the Queen sent him, just as she knew she would!

"Aren't you sweet to come see me, Your Highness. What a pleasant surprise! What can I possibly do for you?" Blizza flutters her lovely eyes. She pulls her shoulders back, displaying alluring curves.

Behind the girl, on her dressing table, amid the bottles

and jars, Clyde glimpses two little rag dolls lying flat, the kind that merchants sell in toy shops. The dolls clearly represent the King and Queen, complete with phony gold crowns that seem to be glowing. Why would she—

Clyde feels a hand, warmly resting on his arm. He looks back to Blizza, who gazes seductively into his eyes. Once again, he feels pleasantly dizzy. "I, uh, just came to tell you that . . ."

His mind is a blank! He can't remember a thing. All he can think of is how nice it would be to kiss this beautiful girl who stands beside him. Does he dare? Well, he is the King, isn't he?

As if reading his mind, Blizza leans closer, rubbing up against his body.

Clyde's lips meet hers in a warm, wonderful kiss . . . just as a solid knock jars the door.

"Blizza! It's Mac. I gotta clean up."

With agonizing slowness, Blizza terminates the kiss. "Later," she whispers. Her breath is hot in Clyde's ear, the lobe of which she maddeningly nibbles. "Meet me here at midnight." She points sideways with a long finger. "On that little pink couch, I will give you great happiness."

She breaks away from Clyde's embrace. "The King is here, you idiot!" she calls. "We were just leaving."

In Broan City, everyone is buzzing about the quake.

"Impending disaster!" says Ira Farwall, a pudgy old man with a rat-tail goatee. His cheeks are covered with thin, red veins—the result of drinking too many "Rusty Spoons" at The Green Lantern. "The imp-flames sunset signaled evil doings, sure as you're born. And the weather is never wrong. That quake could have been much worse, and there's probably more to come."

Mrs. Lili Frizonelli, a thin widow who always wears black, piously objects. "Not if we pray to the O.B.E. Devotion to the O.B.E. overcomes the worst evil, believe you me."

"Poppycrock!" Mr. Farwall snorts. "We'll see whose holy hide gets gored."

FOURTEEN

At eve-meal, the four teenagers are thoughtful. They pick half-heartedly at savory roast duck with glazed sweet potatoes.

Charlton serves them like a silent, cautious ghost.

Even Ruffy, beneath the table, lies fearfully low.

"That was a good rehearsal," Sharoo remarks, glancing at Milli and Bart. "You're totally ready for the performance. Don't you think so, Clyde?"

Clyde seems to be deep in thought.

"Hello, Plash to Clyde! Come in, please."

He shakes his head, refocuses. "Oh, uh, yes. A wonderful performance. Absolutely." He still looks a little dazed. "It was funny. And blizzful." He seems to drift back into some kind of trance.

Sharoo gives him a sharp, penetrating stare. "Are you all right?"

"Absolutely. I'm really looking forward . . . to the performance."

"A lot of weird things have been happening," says Milli, taking a sip of mocha milk. "Poisonous flowers. Vicious puppies. Red rain. The ominous imp-flames sunset . . ."

"Don't forget the plashquake," says Bart. "That really shook me up."

Sharoo smiles uneasily. "Yes, that was weird. I mean, it hit so suddenly. Charlton said it was centered on the theater area."

Milli nods. "It didn't even warn us. Hey, Clyde! Do you think that was what Eeroo meant? Your eyes would see what wasn't there?"

"My eyes?" says Clyde. "My eyes see fine." His dreamy voice sounds furlongs away. His expression is spacey.

Sharoo regards him anxiously, leans closer. "Eeroo's warning. Your eyes would see something that wasn't there."

"Oh, yeah, right," Clyde replies. "I sort of saw the plashquake, but it wasn't really there to see."

Everyone ponders this.

"That could be right," Bart declares, sipping iced zingberry tea. "But we *all* experienced the plashquake, not just Clyde. I have a feeling that whatever Eeroo warned about is yet to come."

Sharoo and Milli shiver.

Clyde shrugs. He still seems a little spacey.

In a corner of the spacious kitchen, Awn whispers: "I heard that the plashquake was conjured up by an evil sorcerer, using purple magic. Nobody knows where he lives, so they can't ketch him." The lad pensively picks his zingberry face.

"Nah," says Auff, sticky fingers ruffling his green hair. "Plashquakes just happen. Totally natural like."

"Not so natural at all," says Awn. "Besides, they say the sorcerer sent a ransack note. By eaglehawk."

Auff gapes. "No Foon farts?"

"I swear by my uncle's glass eye," Awn solemnly declares. "Leastways, that's what I heard." He lowers his voice. "The sorcerer's threatening to make the ground split wide open and swaller the entire castle unless . . ."

"Unless what?"

"Unless the Queen goes to him at midnight, wearing nothing but her ermine overcoat." Awn smiles a wicked smile. "Some of them sorcerers can't get enough of the happy octopus."

Auff squints suspiciously. "Yer fulla cowdroppins," he hisses. "Howz she gonna go to him, if nobody knows where he lives?"

"Uh . . . uh . . ." Awn stammers awkwardly.

Auff has him there.

In her royal bedchamber, wearing Q-S–monogrammed blue-silk pajamas, Sharoo meditates deeply.

After a while, she leans her head back and whispers. "Eedoo! I think I need some help."

Perhaps you do. That was a good meditation.

"Oh, thank the O.B.E. you're communicating! I'm worried about Clyde. He's acting strange, and Eeroo warned him about seeing what isn't there."

I know.

"What should I do? It seems like he's in a trance."

Maybe he is.

Sharoo's eyes grow wide. "How . . . how did it happen? How did he get it? You can't catch a trance like a cold."

In her head, Eedoo makes a mirth-like noise. *No. But someone might have cast a spell.*

"What!?" Sharoo shudders. "Mrs. Zaura is trying to find the sorcerer who is conjuring up puppies and flowers. And she's the only one around here who can cast spells."

Don't be too sure.

"But who? There's no one else . . ."

I can't tell you more. Exercise that lazy brain of yours.

"Can't you give me a clue?"

Silence.

Sharoo thinks desperately for a while, then helplessly shakes her head. She prays and goes to bed.

Almost midnight now. Sharoo tries to sleep, but it's no use. Who could have cast a spell on Clyde? Whoever it was, was probably up to no—

Suddenly, she's wide awake. Blizzful! That's what he said. And Blizza is Mrs. Zaura's granddaughter!

Sharoo races out the door, pokes her head into Clyde's bedchamber. The covers are thrown back. His bed is empty!

He's not in his water room either.

Back in her bedchamber, Sharoo slings off her pajamas. The girl whirls like she's in a speed-dressing contest.

Blizzful!

FIFTEEN

Sharoo dashes down the curving stairs to the darkly gleaming castle door. A tall, burly sentry stands just inside.

"Your Highness! What can I—"

"The King! Did he go out?"

"Why, yes, Your Majesty. He just left. Said he couldn't sleep, needed to get a little fresh—"

"Quick! Open the door. And come with me! Hurry!"

The burly man's eyes bulge. "Yes, Highness."

They dash down the marble steps, but the cold, darkened streets are empty.

Sharoo tilts back her head. "Eedoo!" she whispers.

Silence.

"Follow me!" she tells the guard.

Sharoo runs straight ahead, her eyes desperately probing the empty streets and alleys. The heavy guard pants behind her, his breath making a steamy cloud.

In the shadowy distance, beneath a lamppost, Sharoo spies a short, grubby man raising a bottle to his lips.

She accosts him. "Hey! Did you see the King pass by?"

The man rubs his eyes. "No. I only sheen a few demons."

Sharoo draws herself up, fixes his bleary eyes. "I am your Queen!"

≋

The man gapes and sways. "I, uh . . ."

The guard grabs him by the neck.

"Awk. I remember now. He went thataway." The man points with an unsteady finger. "Forgive me, Your Majeshty. I she things after a few ships. Hic! The King dish-a-peered around that corner . . ."

Sharoo and the guard are already running full speed.

Blizzful! she thinks.

Far ahead, Clyde is hurrying too. The apple-shaped theater draws him like a giant red magnet. His head swirls with visions of Blizza and the little pink couch.

Above him, the great Broan City clock, its hands triumphantly merged, begins to toll midnight.

Clyde climbs the theater steps, two at a time. The heavy door is unlocked, as if it magically expects him. He dashes down the darkened aisle between the silent seats, runs behind the stage to the dressing-room area . . .

At his first knock, an ugly-looking Blizza reactivates her spell. Making hurried mystic signs in the air, she mutters brief, exotic syllables. Ah, that's better!

She trembles pleasantly with the strain. Even with her talent for purple magic, it is difficult to sustain an appearance spell.

The little dressing-room door opens wide.

Clyde, breathing heavily, smiles and stares.

Blizza looks breathlessly beautiful. "Your Majesty! How

lovely!" She draws him inside, smiling slyly. "I knew you would come." She carefully locks the door. "Oh, how I have longed for this moment!"

Clyde dreamily takes her in his arms.

They kiss.

And kiss.

Clyde's world careens wildly. He opens his eyes. For a split second, his head clears. He sees her just as she appeared on the stage!

But only for an instant. Blizza looks lovely once more. Intense passion must have ripped the fabric of reality.

In fact, it did, but with the enchantress. For a moment, her spell had worn thin.

Instantly recovering, a ravishing Blizza gives Clyde a sly, impish grin. "And now, my sweet, as promised, the little pink couch!"

Clyde shivers with anticipation. Yet he hesitates. Deep in his mind, he knows something *isn't quite right.* But he is the King. A wave of lust sweeps over his body. He reaches for Blizza's—

"Open up!" A deep voice sounds outside the door.

Clyde freezes guiltily, his hand outstretched.

Blizza snarls, a hag once more.

With a splintering crash, the door breaks open.

The burly castle guard plunges into the dressing room. Sharoo rushes breathlessly past him.

Quick as a vipersnake, Blizza snatches a dagger from her dressing table.

Sharoo stares in horror. Time seems to freeze, with the slowness of a terrifying nightmare . . .

For an insane instant, the blade flashes in the air like a hovering steel bird. Sharoo dashes forward.

"If I can't have him, no one can!" Blizza plunges the dagger into the center of Clyde's chest, just as Sharoo reaches them.

The sharp blade opens a deep red gash. The wound spurts blood like a gory fountain.

"No!" Sharoo screams. For some strange reason, she recalls the red rain. "No!" Panic turns her cries into wild shrieks. "No!"

The horrible wound still gushes. Clyde's knees buckle. Sharoo tries to hold him up.

Blizza aims her dagger at Sharoo, who fails to notice. She raises her arm . . .

The burly guard restrains the murderess. He twists her arm. The dagger clatters on the floor.

Sharoo staggers, numbly embracing Clyde.

He makes a terrible gurgling sound—and convulsively expires.

Sharoo wails in anguish. With almost superhuman strength, she carries Clyde's body to the little pink couch, gently puts him down, kisses his face. She's drenched in his blood, but doesn't even notice.

Turning fiercely, she glares at Blizza, still held by the strong guard. "Take this creature to the castle dungeon," she gasps. Her lips are trembling. "While I decide how she will die." To Sharoo, her own voice sounds gritty and hard, like someone else's.

"Yes, Your Majesty."

Blizza hisses and spits.

SIXTEEN

Sharoo is devastated. She wanders sobbing through the darkened streets. She doesn't care where she is going, or what happens . . .

From behind, someone roughly grabs her arm.

Startled, she turns.

"Didja find him, Your Highness?" The grubby man grossly belches. "Pardon. I gave yuh the best duh-rek-shuns I could."

With no apparent ill design, he tightens his grip. "Yah look a little red, Highnesh. But I she things . . ."

The Queen gathers a shred of dignity.

"Yes, thank you. I found him . . . but he was busy."

The man's eyes shine in the light of a distant streetlamp. "I shushpected as much, Your Majesty. He looked like he had bishness on his mind." He laughs and hiccups.

Sharoo shakes her arm loose, trudges on, sobbing.

The great castle door is still unlocked. Anyone could enter. Thieves or murderers. She doesn't care.

In her royal bedchamber, with the door locked, Sharoo throws herself on her bed and wails. She beats on the pillows with both fists. She bites her lip until it bleeds.

"Eedoo!" she calls. "Please answer!"

Silence.

How can her Floater *do* that?

Who can help her? Not her parents. Milli? No, she's busy with Bart. Maybe they're in the same room now . . .

Sharoo flinches. The truth is, nobody can do anything. Clyde is gone! He's gone forever. Her sobs grow louder.

She suddenly sits up, desperately hoping that this is a nightmare, and she will soon wake up in this same bed. But she knows that it's not.

Sharoo looks around with empty eyes. Her luxurious room. The rich tapestries, the sofa with gold cushions and ivory tiger-paw legs, the elegantly patterned blue carpet . . . They're all crumbling to dust now.

She calls to Eedoo again. "Please answer, Eedoo! I'll meditate all night if you do."

All right, but that's not necessary. You need some sleep.

"Oh, thank you, *thank* you!" Her voice is shaky. "I felt so alone."

Everyone is alone, except for their Floater.

Sharoo thinks about that. "What can I do, Eedoo? Please tell me!"

Draw upon your inner strength.

"Thanks, but . . . it's hard."

I know. Maybe you should think of someone else.

Sharoo stares. "Who? Clyde is gone, and I don't really care about anyone else."

Maybe you should. Others are suffering too.

"Not as much as I am."

How about Blizza?

Sharoo's wet eyes widen. "Blizza!?" She gasps. "Blizza is

the one who viciously killed him. She stabbed—Oh, no!"
Sharoo shudders. "I *myself* asked Clyde to go to her!"

*That's not what I meant. You also told him the play
might get his mind off making love for a while. But I didn't
mean that either.*

Sharoo stares. How could she have said that to Clyde!

*What I meant was that Blizza is suffering too. She is
in your dungeon, waiting to learn how she will die. Not a
pleasant prospect.*

"But she deserves it."

Remember the Law of Boomerang.

Sharoo stiffens. *Whatever you do comes back to you,* she
automatically thinks. "But . . ."

*But what? What is really in your heart? Are you sure
you want Blizza put to death? She has suffered greatly too.*

Sharoo gapes. "What do you mean?"

*Her frightful appearance. She was mercilessly teased at
school. Children can be very cruel. She has suffered for many
years. At one point, she almost took her own life.*

Sharoo gasps, picturing this. She herself has always been
pretty. She's never thought about what having a repulsive—or
even just unattractive—appearance might be like. She remembers laughing at Blizza's ugly face when Bart, as Delusio,
wooed her on the stage.

"Maybe I won't have her killed."

*Good. She has a Floater too, you know. But as a child,
she turned against it. If you exist, she bitterly thought to
her Floater, why don't you help me not look like this?*

There's a knock at the door. "Your Majesty, it's Charlton."

"Yes?"

"Beg pardon at this hour, Your Highness, but Mrs. Zaura wishes to see you. She said you were awake. It is urgent."

"It's too late!" Sharoo sobs. "Even she can't help me this time!"

Don't be too sure.

Sharoo's eyes grow wide.

She changes her blood-soaked clothes and goes.

SEVENTEEN

When Sharoo knocks, Sniffy doesn't bark. He seems to be as dead as Clyde. She knocks again, limply.

Mrs. Zaura opens the door. No gleaming eyes. No single-tooth grin. She looks haggard and miserable.

Sharoo barely notices. "Clyde is dead!" she blurts, sobbing.

The old lady smiles sadly. "I know. Come in, my dear." She glances up over Sharoo's head. "Hello, Eedoo."

Give her my greetings.

Sharoo gapes. Her Floater has never spoken to anyone else, even indirectly! "Eedoo sends you greetings."

"Thank you, Eedoo." Mrs. Zaura's voice is weak and shaky. To Sharoo she says, "Let's have a hug."

Sharoo is surprised to feel how frail the old woman is. But she finds the thin, shaky arms warm and comforting, as if a loving energy is flowing into her. "Did you . . . see Clyde's death in the crystal?"

"Enough to know." Mrs. Zaura sighs. "I couldn't stop her." She sighs.

"So you know . . . who did it."

"Ah, yes." A tear rolls slowly down her wrinkled face. "I had reached a very special U.R.L."

Sharoo nods. She knows that stands for "Ultra-rarified level."

"Why . . . why did Blizza do it?"

"That's a long story." Mrs. Zaura is breathing hard. "Let's sit down." She motions at her little table.

When they are seated, Mrs. Zaura touches a match to the lone waxlight. Its flame dances in the quarzz crystal.

Sharoo expectantly waits.

The old lady wipes away another tear. Sharoo has never seen her this sad and vulnerable. "I should have stopped her. She was born with badly shaped features, looked sort of like a tiny little hag right from the start. But to her mother Spelza and me, she was winningly cute. We both loved the little scamp. But Spelza couldn't discipline her." She wipes her wrinkled cheek again.

"At school, Blizza was viciously teased. Spelza is quite lovely. The gruesomeness in our line . . . skipped a generation. When Blizza was a young child her teacher, Miss Lurch, told her a little rhyme: *A person who makes fun of you is insecure, and hurting too.* At the time, it seemed to help."

Mrs. Zaura shakes her head. "As she grew up, Blizza fell into a bad crowd, but I didn't suspect purple magic until I saw it."

"Purple magic!" Sharoo's mouth drops open. "I thought only sorcerers practiced purple magic. Did Blizza create the flowers and puppies?"

"I'm afraid so, dearie." Mrs. Zaura sighs.

Sharoo smiles grimly. "Inspector Columbine will be glad to hear that. But how did Blizza learn purple magic?"

"Blizza must have stolen some charms from me, and perverted them." She laughs bitterly. "I'm supposed to be a first-rate seer, but I was blind to someone in my own family."

"You love her," says Sharoo. "It's understandable."

"Thank you. She managed to block me, too." The seer gazes into space. "I know why she chose flowers and puppies to conjure. She was persecuted so much for appearing ugly that she developed a hatred of anything beautiful or cute."

Sharoo nods. "She's a good actress."

"No doubt. But I just now realized how keenly she has suffered. I always thought she managed to shrug off the teasing. She's very strong-willed, like Spelza."

"Could you make her less ugly-looking? Would that help?" Sharoo wonders out loud.

"Maybe," the old woman replies. I'll search for a spell that might do it in a proper way. I should have tried that long ago."

A painful silence fills the room.

Mrs. Zaura frowns. "Blizza is a trippie."

(In Broan City, a trippie is a person who smokes rotweed—a plant that gives rise to fantastic visions but slowly rots the user's brain. The drug has recently become a dangerous fad. Trippies use some words oppositely. "Terrible" means "wonderful," and "fascinating" means "boring.")

Sharoo stares. The room seems to be spinning. Blizza uses purple magic and she's a trippie! "She has a key role in the play."

"I know, dearie." Mrs. Zaura gazes into space. First, she conjured up the flowers and puppies with a powerful spell. Then she enchanted the King."

"I knew it wasn't Clyde's fault!" Sharoo sobs. "I sent him to her myself!"

The old woman nods. "I know you're heartbroken, dearie." She leans closer, eyes gleaming. "There may be a way to save Clyde, but it is fraught with danger."

Sharoo's eyes stretch wide. "S-s-save him!?" she stammers. "But he's dead! I watched him die." She stares at Mrs. Zaura in stunned silence.

EIGHTEEN

Mrs. Zaura gazes into the flickering waxlight and beyond. "Yes, my dear. Clyde is dead in *this* reality. But reality is a little like . . . sweetcrust dough. It can sometimes be molded."

Sharoo jumps up from her chair. "What do you mean?

The old lady grins. Her lone tooth catches the waxlight glow. "To put it a better way, Fate sometimes forks. At rare moments, you can take another branch."

Sharoo sits back down. She leans forward, trembling with excitement. "You mean . . . you mean Clyde can be made alive again?

"Not exactly. But we might be able to *prevent him from dying.* Then, of course, he would still be alive."

Sharoo is speechless. A dead person . . . alive? Her head is spinning. But a beautiful, fragile rainbow of hope arches across her mind. "How could that be done?"

"Sit still a moment."

The old woman rises from her chair. She shuffles over to a dark wooden chest, standing at the foot of her bed. It looks like a weird barrel with iron hoops, lying on its side. Sharoo half expects the chest to be filled with gold coins.

Mrs. Zaura draws a dull brass key from her saggy bosom. It scrapes harshly in the lock.

The lid swings away from the bed, so Sharoo can't see inside.

The old lady shuffles back to the table with a large stack of yellowed parchments. "Spells that belonged to the Wizard Wombler," she croaks. "The ones that have survived. His magic created our strange weather . . . and the wonderfully playful dolphin clouds. Do you remember?"

"Of course!" Sharoo blurts impatiently. "He also created the mango trees, almond bushes, and cinnamon plants."

Mrs. Zaura's lone tooth gleams as she grins. "I see that you do. Well, Wombler left behind some powerful spells. And there are a few I have never tried." She shuffles through the crumbly yellow pages.

Sharoo regards her curiously. Some of the edges are turning to dust.

"Ah! Here we are." The old lady peers down intently. "The spell of fork points."

Sharoo looks blank. "Fork points?"

"Yes, dearie. When Wombler created our strange, spectacular weather, he used his awesome wizardry to weave some permanent interdimensional portals into the fabric of spacetime. These portals are invisible, of course. But with the proper spell, one can access them."

Sharoo looks puzzled. "What for?"

"In case a tragic event occurs. Like King Clyde's death. Something so terrible, it needs to be prevented from happening."

Sharoo gasps. The tiny hairs on the back of her neck stand on end. "Wha—what do you mean?"

Mrs. Zaura's eyes are focused above the Queen's head, beyond Eedoo, far into space. "It may be possible . . . to travel back in spacetime, and alter a small occurrence, so that a major tragedy doesn't happen."

Sharoo's mouth falls open. "That's impossible!"

But, oh, how she wishes it could be done!

"Of course, it is risky," the old lady continues as if Sharoo hadn't spoken. "And it has never been tried before. But now may be the time. Do you know what your star body is?"

Sharoo thinks for a moment. "You mean my Floater?"

"No. This is different. Not a Floater. More like an aura of various colors. A non-physical body that exists on a different plane."

Sharoo gapes.

"Normally a star body is dormant," the seer continues. "But with the right magic spell, it can travel back in spacetime . . . and slightly influence events." She pauses. "Would you be willing to take some great risks . . . to prevent Clyde's death?"

Sharoo jumps up. "Of course! Anything!"

Mrs. Zaura eyes her carefully. "You would leave your flesh body. You would be like the invisible outer skin of a peach, leaving the fruit behind." She pauses ominously. "And you might never return."

Sharoo doesn't hesitate. "My life without Clyde . . . is empty."

"Very well. I shall try to send you back." She gazes into space once more. "Not your physical body, of course, but your star one. Star bodies can travel outside of time and space. Wombler's instructions say to send someone who is in touch with his or her Floater." She sighs. "I've never connected with my Floater. I probably liked gold too much."

Sharoo is lost in thought. "You really mean this, don't you?"

The old woman cackles. "Oh, yes indeed. But the risks are considerable."

"You said that." Sharoo has a suspicious thought. "Why didn't you do this when King Kilgore and Queen Reeya died?"

Mrs. Zaura grins. "Good question, dearie. I considered it. I went into a deep trance, but couldn't find a fork point near their deaths. That made it more unpredictable, more dangerous." She looks deeply into Sharoo's eyes. "You are a Silver Dragon. Your destiny is rare. Let me see if I can locate a fork point not long before Clyde was killed."

Sharoo nods eagerly.

NINETEEN

Sharoo trembles with hope. She watches impatiently as Mrs. Zaura slips into a deep trance. Is the old lady crazy? Wizard Wombler was a very powerful sorcerer, but this spell sounds totally impossible. Way, way far-out!

Like a squadron of scatterbirds, frozen in the sky, the minutes glide excruciatingly by.

(In Broan, these ill-named, long-legged birds actually fly in tight formations. Parents tell young children that scatterbirds bring babies.)

At last, the old lady shakes her head and stretches. "I found a fork point, not too long before Clyde died. The portal was easy to see."

Sharoo jumps up. "Then we can do it?"

"Well, yes. *Your* star body can *attempt* it. But as I said—"

"I know. There are risks." Sharoo is anxious to get going. But a strange thought occurs to her. "If you stay here . . . will you also exist in the past?"

Mrs. Zaura cackles. "Yes. But only as I was then. You won't see me. I wasn't near that fork point." She gazes into space. "But you yourself were, my dear. And your star body, if the spell is successful, can influence your flesh body back then."

The old woman smiles. "All you need to do is concentrate on the past, when you were in the theater and *before* you asked Clyde to go to Blizza. That will help you find the portal. Then you must influence your flesh body to act differently, and return. If you concentrate on the here and now, it should be easy to find the return portal."

Sharoo's eyes grow wide. "What will happen . . . in the past?"

"Your flesh body will act slightly differently . . . and change the course of events. But other happenings will also be altered. The far-reaching consequences of such meddlings are unpredictable."

"Will it be hard to find the portal?"

"Not if you concentrate on the spacetime you are aiming for. You wouldn't want your star body to get stuck in some other wherewhen, hee."

Sharoo sets her jaw. "Let me ask Eedoo's opinion."

"Help yourself, dearie, so to speak."

Sitting quietly, Sharoo tilts back her head, whispers.

"Eedoo! Did you hear what she said?"

Yes.

"Will it work?"

Possibly.

Possibly! Sharoo shudders anxiously. "Will you come too?"

No. I must remain with your flesh body.

"But then I won't have any help!"

If you do this, you must do it without me. The key is to concentrate on the right time and place, as she said.

Sharoo gulps. "What's the worst thing that could happen?

It is better that you do not know. You might give some energy to adverse possibilities.

Sharoo gapes."Is there any other way to bring Clyde back?"

No. But you are young, at an age when star-body travel is easier. An advantage.

"That's nice." Sharoo smiles wryly.

More important, you are an accomplished meditator. And a special Silver Dragon. That should facilitate the procedure.

Sharoo stares bravely into space. "All right. I want to try."

TWENTY

Sharoo watches curiously, anxiously.

Mrs. Zaura mixes magic ingredients with purified water in a glass vial. She shakes it up, places it upright on a little wooden stand. "That must sit for a few minutes," she says.

Now she sprinkles a fine, rainbow-colored powder in a circle on the rug. As she does this, one wrinkled hand makes mystic signs in the air. She mumbles strange words in low tones.

The little trail of powders hisses and smokes.

At last, the old lady breathes with relief. "All right now. Hee. I have an interest in this too, you know. I want to save my granddaughter, misguided as she is. Perhaps she too can be helped, only differently."

Sharoo doesn't ask about that. She's too worried about her own fate. And Clyde's!

"If this is successful," Mrs. Zaura tells her, "the world will change, but we will be the only people who *know* that it has. Everything outside of this circle will be in a different reality, and our magic circle, like a spaceship traveling through spacetime, will have spanned the gap. It will have replaced its counterpart in the altered reality."

Sharoo says absolutely nothing. Words fail her.

"Now, dearie. You must drink this tasty mixture, hee." She

hands Sharoo the glass vial. "It will make you sleepy. We must both meditate inside the circle. You will slip into a dream, but you will be *aware* that you are dreaming. Do not be frightened by anything you think you see."

Sharoo takes a deep breath, gulps down the thick liquid. It tastes like bittersweet cough syrup.

"Now," says Mrs. Zaura.

They both sit in meditation, carefully inside the fateful circle.

After a while, Sharoo slowly drifts off to sleep. She begins to dream, but she is *aware* that she is dreaming, just like Mrs. Zaura said . . .

Now she feels a strange, tingling vibration.

She hears a whistling, whining sound.

She feels "herself" being pulled away from her body! This must be her star body, which she now thinks of as "StarSharoo."

StarSharoo can *see*, even though her flesh body's eyes are closed. She can see herself and Mrs. Zaura, both sitting in the circle. That's amazing!

StarSharoo is not a human girl. Not a ghost either. Her star body is *differently* conscious. This is weirder than weird!

StarSharoo floats freely through the air. Nothing looks like she expected. It's all weird currents and energy swirls. But what did she expect, anyway? Besides, she has . . . a star body's vision.

Now (if that has any meaning) StarSharoo rushes through swirling, churning nonspace. The air is strangely alive. It's eerie, unplashly. She has a mission, but what is it? Oh, yes. The portal. She concentrates on the right place and time . . .

After a timeless flight, she arrives! The portal was easy to find. It's almost as if she has been here before. Very mysterious! She glides effortlessly through. Good! But what is she supposed to do? She tries to remember . . . Oh, yes. StarSharoo needs to influence flesh-body Sharoo NOT to ask Clyde to go to Blizza. It's so simple, but still, it isn't easy . . .

Where is she now? In Speare Theater, so she needs to—

At that moment, something goes wrong. Terribly wrong! The air abruptly shimmers and shakes. StarSharoo tumbles wildly, head over heels. She loses her awareness! Maybe she's dying. Was that one of the risks?

With a superhuman effort, StarSharoo manages to right herself. But who is she?

"Eedoo!" she calls. Then she remembers that her Floater isn't here.

What is she herself doing?

She has absolutely no idea.

TWENTY-ONE

Where is she? What is she doing?

Gradually, StarSharoo regains her awareness. She vaguely understands that she has a mission, but feels totally helpless. Then she has a glimmer of Eedoo's paradox: You must have self-reliance but depend upon a higher power. Self-reliance without ego. She humbly, earnestly prays to the O.B.E.

Almost at once, she feels a dawning realization, remembers what it is that she must do . . .

"Help! It's a plashquake!" Milli screeches.

"That's not the right line," says Bart. But he too is terrified.

Everyone is frozen, braced for another rumbling tremor.

Fortunately, the quake is over as quickly as it hit.

"Whew!" says Clyde. "I thought the theater would collapse."

"Thank the O.B.E. it didn't," says Sharoo, breathing with relief.

Amazingly, there is no damage!

After a few minutes, the rehearsal intrepidly continues.

Into the barroom saunters Allura, a seductress. She is played by a high school student named Blizza. It's amusing because her facial features appear so ugly.

Blizza's yellow-orange skin is dotted with light-brown warts. Her long nose curves down close to thick purple lips. Her eyes glow like hot coals.

"Her makeup is great," whispers Clyde, laughing.

"No makeup," Sharoo tells him. "She's Mrs. Zaura's granddaughter."

Clyde's eyes grow wide.

"I feel sorry for her," Sharoo declares.

On stage, when the Foon spell wears off, Blizza magically enchants Bart, who humorously woos her. Devastated, Loyola wails again. Bart masterfully feigns adoration of Blizza's ugliness.

The play ends when Blizza herself accidentally drinks a love potion and falls in love with the Foon. Bart still pursues Blizza, who is chasing the Foon as the curtain falls.

Sharoo laughs uneasily. She feels sorry for the ugly girl. She wants to ask Clyde to go backstage and tell Blizza what a wonderful actress she is. But somehow, she feels she'd better not. Something . . . bad might happen. She isn't sure what. But she feels so sorry for Blizza! She opens her mouth, but no words come out. It's a strange struggle! A weird feeling. She feels a strong influence NOT to speak. Oh, it must be Eedoo! "Eedoo, is that you?"

Silence.

StarSharoo smiles. Whew! That was the best she could do.

There's an old saying in Broan, "Over easy," meaning it's easy to get something right the second time. But that certainly didn't apply here!

"Now" Sharoo needs to find the return portal.

Mrs. Zaura said to concentrate on the here and now, but it's more like the there and then.

She easily finds the return portal, though.

Still sitting in the circle, Sharoo's flesh body opens its eyes. She feels dreamy, fuzzy, unreal. She sees Mrs. Zaura, watching her intently. "Whuh . . . what happened? I think there was a plashquake."

The old woman cackles softly. "I told you there were risks. But I think you did it, dearie. You were only gone for a few minutes, *in this time*. But it seemed to be enough."

"The plashquake gave me problems." Sharoo's voice is still drowse-fuzzy.

Mrs. Zaura gazes into space for a few moments. "It wasn't a plashquake, dearie. There wasn't any damage."

Sharoo gulps. "What was it?"

"A disruption in the fabric of spacetime, caused by your passing through the portal."

Sharoo thinks back. "That part was easy. The portals seemed strangely familiar."

"That's curious, dearie."

Sharoo suddenly gapes. "Hey! The disruption happened in the past, long before I passed through the portal!"

"Yes. What a delicious paradox!"

Sharoo can't fathom that. She's still a little fuzzy. "My journey didn't seem to take any time. I mean, it did, but it didn't."

"That's because you were in your star body, dearie. You were outside of space and time, even though you were briefly *in* spacetime. Another paradox."

Sharoo feels totally confused now. But she's wide awake.

"Is the magic circle still back in the *other* room?"

Mrs. Zaura cackles. "Who knows? Maybe there's a round hole in the rug. Don't you just love paradoxes?"

Sharoo stares. "What's happening? The room . . . looks blurry!"

"Sit quietly, dearie. Whatever you do, don't leave the circle!"

Sharoo sits like a statue. "But what . . ."

"That's better." The old lady smiles. "There may be one or two more."

"More what?"

"Our circle is still . . . making a landing, dearie. Keep still."

"It didn't seem like we were flying."

"It was in another dimension, dearie. Wombler's spell is winding down."

Sharoo gulps. The room becomes blurry again.

"There, dearie." Mrs. Zaura gazes into the air. "That was the last one."

Sharoo breathes more easily. "Now that I'm back, my flesh body doesn't feel any different."

"Clyde's does."

Sharoo's eyes stretch wide. "He's alive?"

"Go see, hee hee."

"Oh, thank you!" She gives Mrs. Zaura a big hug.

"Hey! My old bones are fragile. But I'm glad you're back, so to speak. You can't imagine what risks there were."

Sharoo, eyes wide, nods. "I don't care now. Where is Clyde?"

"Back here in the cas—"

The Queen is disappearing out the door.

TWENTY-TWO

Sharoo races breathlessly down the curving marble stairs. At the bottom, she almost runs smack into Charlton.

"Beg pardon, Highness. I was just about to dust the—"

"My fault. Where's Clyde?"

"Oh, uh, I believe you'll find the King in the library," Your Highness. "His Majesty said—"

"Thanks!"

Sharoo bursts through the polished wooden door. Clyde is slouched in a large brown armchair, his feet on a hassock, nose in a leather-bound volume.

"Clyde!" She touches his shoulder. It feels solid and warm. He's not dead at all! It worked! She almost faints.

The King looks up. "Oh, hi, Roo. I'm doing some extra reading for Professor Wizzleford. He seemed pretty embarrassed when Milli—"

"You're alive!"

Clyde regards her curiously. "Yeah, last time I checked."

"I'm so glad!"

"So am I." Clyde looks puzzled. "What's up, Roo?"

Sharoo freezes. What should she tell him? How should she begin? This might not be as easy as she thought.

Clyde regards her closely. "What did Mrs. Zaura say? You were with her a long time."

Sharoo's mind swirls. He has absolutely no idea what happened! "She, uh, she was trancing with her crystal. You know how she does. It really didn't seem that long." *That's all completely true,* she thinks.

"Must have been something special."

"All her trancing is special. No one else can do it."

"Of course. But . . . did she figure out the flowers and puppies?"

"Oh, uh, yes. She's going to take care of that."

"Well, who was it? Who is the sorcerer?"

"I . . . can't quite tell you yet." Sharoo sinks down into the adjacent armchair. She suddenly feels wiped, exhausted. "Give me a kiss."

Clyde obliges with alacrity.

It's a good kiss. A wonderful kiss. A better-than-ever kiss. Sharoo happily sighs. It wasn't at all . . . like kissing a corpse!

"Sure you're all right, Roo?"

"Yes. I feel fine. Now, at least. I just . . ."

"Something happened. What was it?"

"I . . . I'll tell you about it later." *After I decide what to say,* she thinks. "Didn't Blizza give a good performance?" she asks.

"I guess so, yeah."

"Give me another kiss."

He leans over eagerly. "When my Queen orders, I must obey."

She kisses him so hard, his eyes bug out. "Hey! What did they put in your mid-meal?"

Sharoo grins. "A passion potion. Like in the play. I fell in love with the first person I saw, and that person was—mmff."

Clyde kisses her right back, equally hard.

Sharoo is giddy with joy. It has never seemed so sweet before!

Something has definitely changed between them. It's not going to be just back to how things were.

TWENTY-THREE

Sharoo slips out through the paneled library door. Shuffling slowly along the hall, she pauses before the staring eyes of previous rulers in gold frames. Queen Reeya seems to look perceptively into her mind. King Kilgore, not so much. She misses them, wondering if she might have seen their spirits on her journey, without recognizing them at all. Everything was so swirly and strange!

Still standing before the portraits, Sharoo takes a deep, grateful breath. She decides not to tell Clyde what she did or why, at least for a while. Her reasoning is tortuous, at best:

If I told him, he'd be ashamed of how he acted—even though it didn't happen, and even though it wasn't his fault when it did happen. After all, he was enchanted by purple magic. Anyway, would he believe me? He might think I'm crazy!

Sharoo finds herself returning to Mrs. Zaura's room. She hesitates, takes a deep breath, and knocks.

The door opens quickly. "Well? Still kicking, isn't he?"

"Yes! I can't thank you enough!" Sharoo smiles. "But I don't know what to tell him."

"That ought to come naturally, hee hee."

Sharoo smiles. "I *did* that. I mean . . . what to tell him about what happened."

The old lady narrows her eyes. "Come in, my dear."

They sit at the familiar table. Waxlight and crystal flicker between them.

Mrs. Zaura sighs. "It's a lot to get used to, isn't it?"

"You know it!" Sharoo nods. "I'm not complaining, though!" She throws up her hands. "It's just so confusing. Clyde will think I'm a loony!"

The old woman cackles like a tickled scruffbird. "You don't have to tell him, you know."

"Yes, but I don't like to keep secre— Hey!" Sharoo's eyes go wide. "What happened to the world where Clyde died? What happened to everyone outside of the magic circle?"

The old woman gazes into space. "Who knows? Maybe they are living on, in their own spacetime continuum. Or maybe they ceased to exist."

Sharoo shudders. "There must be two holes left by you and me . . . in the other reality."

Mrs. Zaura shrugs. "It would be more like a round hole, left by the magic circle. But it's better not to worry about that, hee hee." She lowers her voice. "Did that world collapse, like a balloon with a round hole in it . . . or did it keep on going without us? Who knows? Another mysterious paradox." The old woman sighs. "I wish the Wizard Wombler was here to ask."

Sharoo thinks for a moment. "I hope that other world . . . ceased to exist. There was a lot of suffering in it." *You wouldn't die, but the recovery might be long and painful.* Eedoo's words echo in her mind.

The old woman's eyes glow. She nods, as if she was magically tuned into Sharoo's memory! "I hope it ceased to exist too. But one thing is certain. You and I now exist in this slightly altered reality, where Blizza didn't kill Clyde."

TWENTY-FOUR

Queen Sharoo summons Mother Maura and orders a Service of Gratitude at the temple tomorrow. "For the simple fact that we're alive."

The High Priestess regards her suspiciously but happily. "Yes, gratitude for all our O.B.E.-given blessings." She smiles a smile of bright, beneficent sunbeams. "Fourday is particularly auspicious. G.P.S."

As Sharoo knows, the Priestess means Good Praying Saves. "How about Grateful, Poised, Still?"

Mother Maura's eyes light up. "Oh, Your Highness has thought up a new G.P.S.! May I use that in the temple?"

"Please."

The Priestess puts her palms together in a mastie ("little mast"), bows, and departs.

Next Sharoo orders a very special eve-meal for tonight.

Fat, yellow-skinned Chef Soofull listens carefully.

"There is so little time, Your Highness," he says, twisting his black, shoestring moustache. "Fine food must be prepared with—"

"You'll have more time if you begin *immediately*."

Soofull's eyes widen. "Yes, Highness." He bows and departs.

In her lavish white-marble water room, the Queen takes a hot bath.

After that, she meditates in her bedroom, sitting alertly on a soft gold cushion.

A.S.A.P. Your mind should never lose its magnificent poise.

Sharoo prays gratefully: Clyde is alive, and she herself managed to survive as well. She uses her new G.P.S. Grateful, Poised, Still. Her meditation is long, sweet, and deep.

Well done. Gratitude is a beneficial virtue.

She tilts her head back, smiles. "Eedoo! It's good to have you back. I really missed you."

I know. It's good that . . . StarSharoo is back too.

"Did I come close to failing?"

Only once. Before you overcame your ego, and recalled the paradox of self-reliance but dependence upon a higher power. In your humility, the O.B.E. helped you. In a way, you lost your life in order to find it.

Sharoo's mouth falls open. Like a pale, sudden pearl, a tear rolls down her cheek. "That's why the Wizard Wombler said to send someone in touch with his or her Floater! Mrs. Zaura said he did."

Yes.

"Mrs. Zaura likes paradoxes."

They are useful for attaining humility, insight, and gratitude.

"I'm forever grateful to have Clyde back."

I know. And I see that you are looking forward to exploring what has changed between you. Her Floater puts a small emphasis on the word *changed.*

Sharoo blushes. "Eedoo! Is there anything you don't know?"

Not that you can imagine.

The great dining hall shines with fresh waxlights. The long table is set with the castle's finest linen, gleaming silver, and wedgebone china.

The King and Queen, now actually wearing their gold-trimmed robes, sit beside each other at one end of the lavish banquet table. Their spiky gold crowns sparkle brightly.

Milli and Bart sit on either side. The rest of the table, though covered with a white embroidered cloth, seems almost comically empty and long.

Charlton brings in heavily laden silver trays. Mango soup with dollops of whipped cream. Lemon-puff pastries with caviar inside. Fragrant, sumptuous roast pheasant. Marshmallow mashed potatoes. Rich, snoot-flavored gravy. Brown-sugar-glazed peas. Goblets of zingberry wine.

Bart whistles. "This is a meal . . . fit for a king!"

Milli giggles.

Sharoo and Clyde laugh.

Below the banquet table, Ruffy happily munches crispy bacon strips from a gold-plated bowl.

Seen from above, four silver forks, attached to four hands and arms, shovel food into four human faces.

Three of the four talk in low, relieved tones about the plashquake.

Sharoo listens carefully. They think it really was a quake. And, of course, they think there was only one.

"Really shook me up," says Bart.

"I think you said that before," Milli tells him uncertainly. She takes a sip of zingberry wine. "Maybe we're in a repeating time loop!" She laughs, her beady eyes shining. "That would make a great science fiction story!"

Sharoo *doesn't* laugh.

"I'm glad nobody was hurt," says Clyde. "That plashquake was powerful. It made me feel how fragile our lives really are."

Sharoo nods. "You have no idea," she enigmatically remarks.

Clyde gives her a strange look. She's acting a little weird, he thinks. The waxlights create a warm, romantic glow.

As Clyde surmised, Sharoo is hazedreaming too. She wonders if it's as wonderful as some people say . . .

In her little room, after a light supper, Mrs. Zaura feverishly magicks. On her work table, pungent vapors rise from twin beakers atop small metal burners. Bunches of rare herbs lie nearby. Beside them stretches a yellowed parchment scroll, its crumbling corners pinned down by bottles and jars. The witch-like seer has found the Wombler spell she was seeking!

In her own way, the old woman gratefully thanks the O.B.E. She works far into the night . . .

Well done. The voice murmurs softly in her head. The seer's misty eyes widen with surprise.

She thinks for a few moments, trembling slightly. "May I call you Eebliz?"

Yes.

The next morning, Sharoo and Clyde awaken in the Queen's luxurious bed, happy and relaxed.

In another part of Broan City, Blizza suddenly awakens. She yawns, leaps, floats to the floor. Shuffling to her water room, she stares, wide-eyed, at the perfectly normal face in the mirror.

Not ugly. Not ravishingly beautiful. Just blissfully normal.

Below her shiny image blinks the message:

Come see me. —Grams.

EPILOGUE

Throughout Broan City, the evil flowers and vicious puppies suddenly vanish. And cease to appear.

Inspector Columbine modestly refuses to say how he solved the mysterious case—and put an end to the terrible purple magic.

When a normal-looking Blizza obeys the magical instruction in the mirror, her grandmother receives her warmly. But there is an awkward silence. After a while, Mrs. Zaura convinces the girl to stop smoking rotweed. And to stop practicing purple magic. "I'll know," she tells the frowning girl. "And I'll send for you soon."

Blizza nods. "Thank you again for the transformation, Grams."

What will Mrs. Zaura tell the detoxified girl? That surface beauty is, well, superficial. That Blizza must learn to appreciate *inner* beauty. That her skill with magic and influencing mindmake is something to treasure, something that can be used to help others. That instead of trying to gain more power to fool people and make things appear that aren't real, she can use it to help people see what is real beneath superficial appearances. That as she learns to focus on the beauty *within*, it will radiate through her. And that will be what people worth knowing will see in her no matter what her physical features are like.

Before long, Blizza will persuade some of her trippie friends to kick their rotweed addictions. It will be a lengthy, but gratifying endeavor . . .

The special reserve mango brandy is now locked in the royal wine cellar. (After Auff clumsily spilled a tray of empty dishes in Mrs. Zaura's room, she tranced, and told the Queen why.) Now, only Sharoo and Charlton have wine-cellar keys.

So far, Queen Sharoo hasn't brought herself to tell Clyde what really "happened." She can't think of how to put it, and wonders if he'd think she's crazy. Anyway, what good would it do? *You don't have to tell him, you know.* Mrs. Zaura's words echo in Sharoo's memory.

Mrs. Zaura herself keeps wondering about the fate of the "reality" in which Clyde died. Did it continue, or did it cease to exist? The question haunts her. It's like a sharp splinter in her wrinkled skin.

When the old seer attempts to contact Wizard Wombler's spirit, she encounters nothing but emptiness. But she does intuit a startling insight. Wombler, she strongly suspects, was reborn as the Silver Dragon Sharoo Loo! When Sharoo's star body traveled through his portals, they "seemed strangely familiar." In a sense, he was utilizing his own magical constructions!

No wonder the girl remembered so clearly the things that Wombler did for Plash. "He also created the mango trees, almond bushes, and cinnamon plants," Sharoo said. Why did she seem so in tune with the Wizard, unless she knew, at some level, what he had done?

The seer's mind flashes back three years to when Sharoo, facing the evil Morfers, invented a tale that the Wizard Wombler created a magic spell to protect the planet. That tale had saved Plash! At the time, it seemed like a clever, resourceful fantasy. And no doubt it was. The old lady gasps. Is it possible that Wombler actually created that spell?

She closes her eyes, whispers. "Eebliz, is my suspicion that Wombler was reborn as Sharoo correct?"

Yes.

"Thank you." She smiles. "Did the Wizard create a spell to protect Plash?"

Yes.

"Was there an invading race called Zlobers?"

No. Sharoo made them up, based on something her friend Milli Potch read in Mind-Chilling Speculations.

Mrs. Zaura nods. "Is Wombler's protection spell still in effect?"

No. It wore thin many years ago.

The old lady's eyes grow wide. Sharoo's clever bluff stopped the Morfers after all! "Can the spell . . . be reactivated?"

No. Wombler expected it to last. His magic was awesome, but not perfect.

Mrs. Zaura thinks for a moment. "Eebliz! What happened to the reality in which Clyde died?"

That is hard to explain. Your mind will best understand that your present reality is the only surviving one.

The old seer smiles with relief. That seems good enough. Her thoughts return to Sharoo. The girl is an incarnation of

Wombler. What will she think about that? But should she be told? The old seer recalls Queen Quist, the only other Silver Dragon in recorded history. "Puffed up with pride, the great Quist died," Broanians say.

She closes her eyes again. "Should I tell Sharoo?"

Silence.

But an old saying pops into her mind. "Keep a secret, and it won't bite."